DreamWorks®

MADAGASCAR 3

MAD LIBS®

concept created by Roger Price & Leonard Stern

PSS!

PRICE STERN SLOAN

An Imprint of Penguin Group (USA) Inc.

PRICE STERN SLOAN
Published by the Penguin Group
Penguin Group (USA) Inc., 375 Hudson Street, New York, New York 10014, USA
Penguin Group (Canada), 90 Eglinton Avenue East, Suite 700,
Toronto, Ontario M4P 2Y3, Canada
(a division of Pearson Penguin Canada Inc.)
Penguin Books Ltd., 80 Strand, London WC2R 0RL, England
Penguin Group Ireland, 25 St. Stephen's Green, Dublin 2, Ireland
(a division of Penguin Books Ltd.)
Penguin Group (Australia), 250 Camberwell Road, Camberwell, Victoria 3124, Australia
(a division of Pearson Australia Group Pty. Ltd.)
Penguin Books India Pvt. Ltd., 11 Community Centre,
Panchsheel Park, New Delhi—110 017, India
Penguin Group (NZ), 67 Apollo Drive, Rosedale, Auckland 0632, New Zealand
(a division of Pearson New Zealand Ltd.)
Penguin Books (South Africa) (Pty.) Ltd., 24 Sturdee Avenue,
Rosebank, Johannesburg 2196, South Africa

Penguin Books Ltd., Registered Offices:
80 Strand, London WC2R 0RL, England

ISBN 978-0-8431-6998-0

3 5 7 9 10 8 6 4

ALWAYS LEARNING   PEARSON

MAD LIBS
INSTRUCTIONS

MAD LIBS® is a game for people who don't like games!
It can be played by one, two, three, four, or forty.

• RIDICULOUSLY SIMPLE DIRECTIONS

In this tablet you will find stories containing blank spaces where words
are left out. One player, the READER, selects one of these stories. The
READER does not tell anyone what the story is about. Instead, he/she asks
the other players, the WRITERS, to give him/her words. These words are
used to fill in the blank spaces in the story.

• TO PLAY

The READER asks each WRITER in turn to call out a word—an adjective or
a noun or whatever the space calls for—and uses them to fill in the blank
spaces in the story. The result is a MAD LIBS® game.

When the READER then reads the completed MAD LIBS® game to the other
players, they will discover that they have written a story that is fantastic,
screamingly funny, shocking, silly, crazy, or just plain dumb—depending
upon which words each WRITER called out.

• EXAMPLE (*Before* and *After*)

"_____ !" he said _____
        EXCLAMATION   ADVERB

as he jumped into his convertible _____ and
                                                      NOUN

drove off with his _____ wife.
                              ADJECTIVE

"_____*Ouch*_____ !" he said _____*stupidly*_____
        EXCLAMATION   ADVERB

as he jumped into his convertible _____*cat*_____ and
                                             NOUN

drove off with his _____*brave*_____ wife.
                          ADJECTIVE

MAD LIBS®
QUICK REVIEW

In case you have forgotten what adjectives, adverbs, nouns, and verbs are, here is a quick review:

An ADJECTIVE describes something or somebody. *Lumpy*, *soft*, *ugly*, *messy*, and *short* are adjectives.

An ADVERB tells how something is done. It modifies a verb and usually ends in "ly." *Modestly*, *stupidly*, *greedily*, and *carefully* are adverbs.

A NOUN is the name of a person, place, or thing. *Sidewalk*, *umbrella*, *bridle*, *bathtub*, and *nose* are nouns.

A VERB is an action word. *Run*, *pitch*, *jump*, and *swim* are verbs. Put the verbs in past tense if the directions say PAST TENSE. *Ran*, *pitched*, *jumped*, and *swam* are verbs in the past tense.

When we ask for A PLACE, we mean any sort of place: a country or city (*Spain*, *Cleveland*) or a room (*bathroom*, *kitchen*).

An EXCLAMATION or SILLY WORD is any sort of funny sound, gasp, grunt, or outcry, like *Wow!*, *Ouch!*, *Whomp!*, *Ick!*, and *Gadzooks!*

When we ask for specific words, like a NUMBER, a COLOR, an ANIMAL, or a PART OF THE BODY, we mean a word that is one of those things, like *seven*, *blue*, *horse*, or *head*.

When we ask for a PLURAL, it means more than one. For example, *cat* pluralized is *cats*.

MAD LIBS® is fun to play with friends, but you can also play it by yourself! To begin with, DO NOT look at the story on the page below. Fill in the blanks on this page with the words called for. Then, using the words you have selected, fill in the blank spaces in the story.

Now you've created your own hilarious MAD LIBS® game!

NYC OR BUST

PLURAL NOUN _____

ADJECTIVE _____

PLURAL NOUN _____

NOUN _____

PART OF THE BODY _____

PLURAL NOUN _____

NOUN _____

NOUN _____

NOUN _____

PART OF THE BODY _____

NOUN _____

A PLACE _____

ADJECTIVE _____

ADJECTIVE _____

PLURAL NOUN _____

MAD LIBS®
NYC OR BUST

Many _____ ago, some animals escaped from the New York
         PLURAL NOUN

Zoo. They went on a/an _____ journey to Madagascar and
                              ADJECTIVE

the African Sahara, making new _____ along the way.
                                      PLURAL NOUN

But now all they want is to go home to the Big _____.
                                                      NOUN

Alex the lion has a/an _____ of gold and a mane of
                        PART OF THE BODY

_____.
   PLURAL NOUN

Marty the zebra is as curious as a/an _____; he's
                                              NOUN

always up for a new _____.
                          NOUN

Gloria, the sassy hippopotamus, and **Melman**, the nervous giraffe, are

as different as night and _____—but they're joined at
                                NOUN

the _____.
      PART OF THE BODY

The chimps, **Phil** and **Mason**, are smarter than the average _____.
                                                                  NOUN

King Julien, the lemur with an ego the size of (the) _____,
                                                         A PLACE

hails from Madagascar as do his _____ servants, **Mort**
                                      ADJECTIVE

and **Maurice**.

The Penguins, **Skipper**, **Rico**, **Kowalski**, and **Private** always have a/an

_____ scheme up their _____.
      ADJECTIVE   PLURAL NOUN

From MADAGASCAR 3 MAD LIBS®. Madagascar 3 © 2012 DreamWorks Animation L.L.C. Published by
Price Stern Sloan, an imprint of Penguin Group (USA) Inc., 345 Hudson Street, New York, NY 10014.

MAD LIBS® is fun to play with friends, but you can also play it by yourself! To begin with, DO NOT look at the story on the page below. Fill in the blanks on this page with the words called for. Then, using the words you have selected, fill in the blank spaces in the story.

Now you've created your own hilarious MAD LIBS® game!

I HEART NEW YORK

NOUN _____

NOUN _____

PART OF THE BODY _____

NOUN _____

PLURAL NOUN _____

PART OF THE BODY _____

NOUN _____

VERB _____

PLURAL NOUN _____

ADJECTIVE _____

NOUN _____

ADVERB _____

NOUN _____

EXCLAMATION _____

NOUN _____

MAD LIBS

I HEART NEW YORK

After years away from the New York Zoo, the gang wants nothing

more than to return to the New York _____. When
                                          NOUN

asked why they want to go home, here's how they responded:

Alex: "Sure, the lion is _____ of the jungle, but I need
                                   NOUN

to get my _____ back to the *concrete* jungle where I
              PART OF THE BODY

rule the _____."
              NOUN

Mason: "Ugh, these wild _____ are so uncivilized!
                                PLURAL NOUN

My _____ yearns for the _____ of the big city!"
      PART OF THE BODY   NOUN

Skipper: "The New York Zoo can't _____ without me
                                          VERB

and my flippered _____! Only my compadres and I
                      PLURAL NOUN

can whip that _____ sardine can into shape!"
                    ADJECTIVE

King Julien: "I have not been to this New York thingima-

_____, but I hear the New York peoples like to party
      NOUN

_____ and shake their _____-makers!
      ADVERB   NOUN

_____! I hope the _____ that never sleeps
EXCLAMATION   NOUN

is ready for this jelly!"

From MADAGASCAR 3 MAD LIBS®. Madagascar 3 © 2012 DreamWorks Animation L.L.C. Published by
Price Stern Sloan, an imprint of Penguin Group (USA) Inc., 345 Hudson Street, New York, NY 10014.

MAD LIBS® is fun to play with friends, but you can also play it by yourself! To begin with, DO NOT look at the story on the page below. Fill in the blanks on this page with the words called for. Then, using the words you have selected, fill in the blank spaces in the story.

Now you've created your own hilarious MAD LIBS® game!

MONTE CARLO MISCHIEF

VERB ENDING IN "S" _____

NOUN _____

PLURAL NOUN _____

PLURAL NOUN _____

NOUN _____

NOUN _____

ADJECTIVE _____

NOUN _____

PLURAL NOUN _____

ADJECTIVE _____

NOUN _____

ADJECTIVE _____

PART OF THE BODY _____

PART OF THE BODY _____

TYPE OF LIQUID _____

NOUN _____

NOUN _____

MAD LIBS®
MONTE CARLO MISCHIEF

What happens in Monte Carlo _____ in Monte Carlo.
                            VERB ENDING IN "S"

Phil, Mason, and the Penguins are living in the _____
                                                NOUN

of luxury, winning thousands of _____ at the Monte
                                 PLURAL NOUN

Carlo Casino and spending them all on delicious fish, bananas, and

luxury _____. Their five-_____ hotel
        PLURAL NOUN   NOUN

room at the Hotel de _____, a/an _____
                      NOUN   ADJECTIVE

suite fit for a/an _____, is littered with banana peels,
                   NOUN

old _____, and feathers from pillow fights of
     PLURAL NOUN

_____ proportions. It's a nightmare for the cleaning
 ADJECTIVE

_____. But because they're high rollers, the Chimps
 NOUN

and Penguins get _____ treatment. When they're not
                  ADJECTIVE

gambling, pillow fighting, and eating to their _____'s
                                                PART OF THE BODY

delight, they're getting _____ massages at the hotel spa
                          PART OF THE BODY

or going for a dip in the warm _____-filled pool. It's a/an
                                TYPE OF LIQUID

_____ come true. But can a/an _____
 NOUN   NOUN

like this last forever?

MAD LIBS® is fun to play with friends, but you can also play it by yourself! To begin with, DO NOT look at the story on the page below. Fill in the blanks on this page with the words called for. Then, using the words you have selected, fill in the blank spaces in the story.

Now you've created your own hilarious MAD LIBS® game!

THE KING OF VERSAILLES

NOUN _____

NOUN _____

PART OF THE BODY _____

NOUN _____

PLURAL NOUN _____

NOUN _____

NOUN _____

PERSON IN ROOM _____

PLURAL NOUN _____

NOUN _____

NOUN _____

PERSON IN ROOM (FEMALE) _____

ADJECTIVE _____

NOUN _____

PLURAL NOUN _____

MAD LIBS®
THE KING OF VERSAILLES

Just who is the mystery _____ who's been taking Monte

NOUN

Carlo by storm? That's the question on every _____'s

NOUN

_____. The so-called King of Versailles has been

PART OF THE BODY

sweeping the tables at the famed _____ Casino, leaving

NOUN

with pockets full of _____. The odd thing is, no

PLURAL NOUN

one knows where this _____ comes from. "He just

NOUN

waltzed in one day and plunked his _____ down on

NOUN

a table," casino manager _____ said. But even though

PERSON IN ROOM

the King of Versailles is rolling in _____, he keeps

PLURAL NOUN

a pretty low profile. "He doesn't say much," said one card dealer.

"As a matter of fact, I don't think I've ever heard him make a/an

_____." "He seems like a nice _____," added

NOUN   NOUN

waitress _____. "And he's a very _____

PERSON IN ROOM (FEMALE)   ADJECTIVE

tipper." One thing's for sure: This high-rolling _____ has

NOUN

Lady Luck on his side. Sources say he's earned more than one million

_____.

PLURAL NOUN

From MADAGASCAR 3 MAD LIBS®. Madagascar 3 © 2012 DreamWorks Animation L.L.C. Published by
Price Stern Sloan, an imprint of Penguin Group (USA) Inc., 345 Hudson Street, New York, NY 10014.

MAD LIBS® is fun to play with friends, but you can also play it by yourself! To begin with, DO NOT look at the story on the page below. Fill in the blanks on this page with the words called for. Then, using the words you have selected, fill in the blank spaces in the story.

Now you've created your own hilarious MAD LIBS® game!

ON THE RUN

NOUN _____

ADJECTIVE _____

NOUN _____

PART OF THE BODY _____

NUMBER _____

NOUN _____

PLURAL NOUN _____

PLURAL NOUN _____

PLURAL NOUN _____

ADVERB _____

A PLACE _____

VERB _____

PLURAL NOUN _____

PART OF THE BODY (PLURAL) _____

ADJECTIVE _____

NOUN _____

VERB _____

MAD LIBS

ON THE RUN

NEWSFLASH: Monte Carlo residents, be on _____

<u>NOUN</u>

alert—a group of _____ animals is on the loose

<u>ADJECTIVE</u>

this evening. Reports say a pack of animals appeared out of thin

_____ inside the Monte Carlo Casino. According to

<u>NOUN</u>

_____-witnesses, a hippopotamus, a lion, a giraffe,

<u>PART OF THE BODY</u>

a zebra, and at least _____ penguins and chimpanzees

<u>NUMBER</u>

knocked over _____ tables, smashed _____,

<u>NOUN</u>   <u>PLURAL NOUN</u>

and frightened casino _____ away. No _____

<u>PLURAL NOUN</u>   <u>PLURAL NOUN</u>

were harmed, but the animals _____ escaped the casino

<u>ADVERB</u>

and are now thought to be headed to (the) _____.

<u>A PLACE</u>

We'd like to remind you to please _____ with caution.

<u>VERB</u>

All _____ are encouraged to stay indoors. Keep

<u>PLURAL NOUN</u>

your _____ peeled and stay alert at all times. If

<u>PART OF THE BODY (PLURAL)</u>

you happen to spot one of these _____ creatures, please

<u>ADJECTIVE</u>

call Monte Carlo _____ Control immediately. And

<u>NOUN</u>

whatever you do, stay calm and don't _____.

<u>VERB</u>

From MADAGASCAR 3 MAD LIBS®. Madagascar 3 © 2012 DreamWorks Animation L.L.C. Published by
Price Stern Sloan, an imprint of Penguin Group (USA) Inc., 345 Hudson Street, New York, NY 10014.

MAD LIBS® is fun to play with friends, but you can also play it by yourself! To begin with, DO NOT look at the story on the page below. Fill in the blanks on this page with the words called for. Then, using the words you have selected, fill in the blank spaces in the story.

Now you've created your own hilarious MAD LIBS® game!

THE CIRCUS CLAN

ADJECTIVE _____

ADJECTIVE _____

A PLACE _____

ADJECTIVE _____

ADJECTIVE _____

PLURAL NOUN _____

ADJECTIVE _____

ADJECTIVE _____

ADJECTIVE _____

PART OF THE BODY _____

NOUN _____

ADJECTIVE _____

NOUN _____

ADJECTIVE _____

PART OF THE BODY _____

ADJECTIVE _____

VERB ENDING IN "ING" _____

MAD LIBS

THE CIRCUS CLAN

When the Zoosters escaped Capitain Dubois's _____

ADJECTIVE

clutches, they stumbled upon a/an _____ circus train.

ADJECTIVE

When they were reluctantly let aboard the _____-

A PLACE

bound train, they met these _____ creatures:

ADJECTIVE

Vitaly is a/an _____ Russian tiger who does not

ADJECTIVE

mince his _____. This _____ cat sure can

PLURAL NOUN   ADJECTIVE

be a sourpuss, but beneath his _____ exterior, he's just

ADJECTIVE

a wounded, _____ soul.

ADJECTIVE

Stefano, on the other _____, is quite the upbeat

PART OF THE BODY

sea lion. This Italian _____ is a glass-is-always-

NOUN

half-_____ kind of guy who knows how to look on

ADJECTIVE

the _____ side of life.

NOUN

Gia is a breathtakingly _____ jaguar with a warm and

ADJECTIVE

giving _____. She has a/an _____ imagination

PART OF THE BODY   ADJECTIVE

and can often be found daydreaming about _____.

VERB ENDING IN "ING"

From MADAGASCAR 3 MAD LIBS®. Madagascar 3 © 2012 DreamWorks Animation L.L.C. Published by Price Stern Sloan, an imprint of Penguin Group (USA) Inc., 345 Hudson Street, New York, NY 10014.

MAD LIBS® is fun to play with friends, but you can also play it by yourself! To begin with, DO NOT look at the story on the page below. Fill in the blanks on this page with the words called for. Then, using the words you have selected, fill in the blank spaces in the story.

Now you've created your own hilarious MAD LIBS® game!

TERRIFYING TERRIERS

ADJECTIVE _____

NOUN _____

VERB ENDING IN "ING" _____

ADJECTIVE _____

ADJECTIVE _____

PART OF THE BODY _____

ADJECTIVE _____

NOUN _____

NOUN _____

NOUN _____

ADJECTIVE _____

VERB _____

NOUN _____

NOUN _____

PLURAL NOUN _____

MAD LIBS®

TERRIFYING TERRIERS

Oy, gov'na! Yeah, you, you _____ _____ .
                                ADJECTIVE   NOUN

Are you _____ at me? Something wrong with what
         VERB ENDING IN "ING"

you see, is there? What? You think I'm just an _____ ,
                                                 ADJECTIVE

adorable puppy wearing my wee, _____ tutu, now do
                                 ADJECTIVE

ya? Well I ought to give you a piece of my _____ ,
                                            PART OF THE BODY

I ought. I don't go around *ooh*ing and *aah*ing and talking like a/an

_____ baby when I see *you*. That would be daft, now
  ADJECTIVE

wouldn't it? So what makes you think you can go ahead and treat me

like a cute, little _____ ? I'm not a stuffed _____ ,
                    NOUN   NOUN

you know. I'm a tough _____ —and, though I might be
                       NOUN

_____ , I know how to _____ like a big dog.
  ADJECTIVE   VERB

You get my _____ , mate? All right, then. Now naff off,
            NOUN

ya _____ . I've got bigger _____ to fry.
    NOUN   PLURAL NOUN

MAD LIBS® is fun to play with friends, but you can also play it by yourself! To begin with, DO NOT look at the story on the page below. Fill in the blanks on this page with the words called for. Then, using the words you have selected, fill in the blank spaces in the story.

Now you've created your own hilarious MAD LIBS® game!

ROMAN HOLIDAY

PART OF THE BODY (PLURAL) _____

NOUN _____

NOUN _____

ADJECTIVE _____

NOUN _____

NOUN _____

PART OF THE BODY (PLURAL) _____

PLURAL NOUN _____

NOUN _____

PART OF THE BODY (PLURAL) _____

PART OF THE BODY (PLURAL) _____

NOUN _____

NOUN _____

PART OF THE BODY (PLURAL) _____

NOUN _____

ADJECTIVE _____

NOUN _____

MAD ◉ LIBS®
ROMAN HOLIDAY

When King Julien set _____ on Sonya the
PART OF THE BODY (PLURAL)

bear, it was love at first _____. Before Sonya could say
NOUN

"_____," Julien whisked her off on a whirlwind date
NOUN

around the _____ city of Rome. Perched atop Sonya's
ADJECTIVE

bicycle, the two wheeled their way to the Vatican, where Julien

took the Pope's _____, giving it to Sonya as a promise
NOUN

of his undying _____. Next they visited the Roman
NOUN

Forum, where they scratched their _____ on
PART OF THE BODY (PLURAL)

ancient _____. When Sonya accidentally smashed her
PLURAL NOUN

bicycle, Julien got her a brand-new motor-_____. The
NOUN

two zoomed around Rome, the wind in their _____
PART OF THE BODY (PLURAL)

and the sun on their _____. Finally they stopped at
PART OF THE BODY (PLURAL)

an Italian _____ where they fed each other spaghetti
NOUN

with _____-balls. Their _____ full and their
NOUN   PART OF THE BODY (PLURAL)

hearts bursting with _____, Julien and Sonya's first date
NOUN

came to a/an _____ end—but their _____
ADJECTIVE   NOUN

was just beginning.

From MADAGASCAR 3 MAD LIBS®. Madagascar 3 © 2012 DreamWorks Animation L.L.C. Published by
Price Stern Sloan, an imprint of Penguin Group (USA) Inc., 345 Hudson Street, New York, NY 10014.

MAD LIBS® is fun to play with friends, but you can also play it by yourself! To begin with, DO NOT look at the story on the page below. Fill in the blanks on this page with the words called for. Then, using the words you have selected, fill in the blank spaces in the story.

Now you've created your own hilarious MAD LIBS® game!

DUBOIS DOSSIER

ADJECTIVE _____

A PLACE _____

PART OF THE BODY (PLURAL) _____

PERSON IN ROOM (FEMALE) _____

ADJECTIVE _____

ADJECTIVE _____

PLURAL NOUN _____

ADJECTIVE _____

NOUN _____

VERB _____

NOUN _____

NOUN _____

NOUN _____

NUMBER _____

NOUN _____

ADJECTIVE _____

NOUN _____

MAD LIBS

DUBOIS DOSSIER

The following is a/an _____ confidential document
                        ADJECTIVE

belonging to the national police of (the) _____. It is
                                          A PLACE

for official police _____ only.
                    PART OF THE BODY (PLURAL)

Name: Capitain _____ Dubois
                    PERSON IN ROOM (FEMALE)

Occupation: _____ Animal Control specialist
                 ADJECTIVE

with a focus on _____ game such as lions, tigers,
                  ADJECTIVE

and _____
     PLURAL NOUN

Skills: a super-_____ sense of smell akin to that of a/an
                     ADJECTIVE

_____-hound and the ability to _____
    NOUN   VERB

faster than a speeding _____.
                          NOUN

Accomplishments: was voted Most Likely to Wrestle a/an _____ in
                                                              NOUN

her police academy class, recipient of the _____ Controller of
                                              NOUN

the Year award _____ years in a row.
                  NUMBER

Notes: Take caution: Capitain Dubois is a talented and determined

_____, but she has a/an _____ temper. Cross
    NOUN   ADJECTIVE

her at your own _____.
                   NOUN

From MADAGASCAR 3 MAD LIBS®. Madagascar 3 © 2012 DreamWorks Animation L.L.C. Published by
Price Stern Sloan, an imprint of Penguin Group (USA) Inc., 345 Hudson Street, New York, NY 10014.

MAD LIBS® is fun to play with friends, but you can also play it by yourself! To begin with, DO NOT look at the story on the page below. Fill in the blanks on this page with the words called for. Then, using the words you have selected, fill in the blank spaces in the story.

Now you've created your own hilarious MAD LIBS® game!

STEP RIGHT UP!

PLURAL NOUN _____

PART OF THE BODY (PLURAL) _____

PLURAL NOUN _____

PLURAL NOUN _____

PLURAL NOUN _____

PLURAL NOUN _____

NOUN _____

NOUN _____

PART OF THE BODY _____

PLURAL NOUN _____

ADJECTIVE _____

ADJECTIVE _____

NOUN _____

NOUN _____

PART OF THE BODY _____

NOUN _____

ADJECTIVE _____

A PLACE _____

MAD LIBS
STEP RIGHT UP!

Step right up, girls and _____, to see the Circus Zaragoza!

PLURAL NOUN

Your _____ will be amazed at the _____

PART OF THE BODY (PLURAL)   PLURAL NOUN

you're about to see! Yes, for just five _____ you can see

PLURAL NOUN

_____ balancing on rubber _____! A sea

PLURAL NOUN   PLURAL NOUN

_____ who can juggle a/an _____ on the tip

NOUN   NOUN

of his _____! Tiny, little dancing _____! And

PART OF THE BODY   PLURAL NOUN

the most _____ sight you've ever seen: a/an _____

ADJECTIVE   ADJECTIVE

lion jumping through a teeny, tiny flaming _____. It's

NOUN

truly _____-defying! Don't believe the words that are

NOUN

coming out of my _____? Buy a/an _____

PART OF THE BODY   NOUN

and see for yourself! Circus Zaragoza is the most _____

ADJECTIVE

show in (the) _____!

A PLACE

From MADAGASCAR 3 MAD LIBS®. Madagascar 3 © 2012 DreamWorks Animation L.L.C. Published by
Price Stern Sloan, an imprint of Penguin Group (USA) Inc., 345 Hudson Street, New York, NY 10014.

MAD LIBS® is fun to play with friends, but you can also play it by yourself! To begin with, DO NOT look at the story on the page below. Fill in the blanks on this page with the words called for. Then, using the words you have selected, fill in the blank spaces in the story.

Now you've created your own hilarious MAD LIBS® game!

CIRQUE DU *SO* LAME, BY ALEX

VERB _____

ADJECTIVE _____

PLURAL NOUN _____

NOUN _____

A PLACE _____

NOUN _____

ADJECTIVE _____

PART OF THE BODY _____

PLURAL NOUN _____

VERB ENDING IN "ING" _____

PART OF THE BODY (PLURAL) _____

PLURAL NOUN _____

ADJECTIVE _____

NOUN _____

ADJECTIVE _____

NOUN _____

VERB _____

I was so excited to see the Circus Zaragoza perform, I could

hardly _____. We had just bought the circus from their
                VERB

_____ owners. The plan was to make our way to London,
   ADJECTIVE

where the circus would impress the _____ off an American
                                        PLURAL NOUN

circus promoter. Hopefully it would be a one-way _____
                                                        NOUN

home to (the) _____. So when it turned out that Stefano
                 A PLACE

couldn't juggle a/an _____ to save his life and that Vitaly
                         NOUN

was too _____ to jump through a hoop, I felt panic rising
            ADJECTIVE

in my _____. The horses were eating _____
         PART OF THE BODY   PLURAL NOUN

instead of _____ like they were supposed to. The
              VERB ENDING IN "ING"

dancing dogs chased their own _____ instead
                                    PART OF THE BODY (PLURAL)

of dancing. And the elephants' attempts to balance on rubber

_____ ended in disaster when one _____ audience
   PLURAL NOUN   ADJECTIVE

member blew a spit-_____ at them. Afterward, we barely
                        NOUN

escaped a/an _____ mob wanting its _____ back. If we're
                ADJECTIVE   NOUN

ever going to get home, we'll need to shape up or _____ out.
                                                        VERB

MAD LIBS® is fun to play with friends, but you can also play it by yourself! To begin with, DO NOT look at the story on the page below. Fill in the blanks on this page with the words called for. Then, using the words you have selected, fill in the blank spaces in the story.

Now you've created your own hilarious MAD LIBS® game!

ODE TO SONYA

NOUN _____

PART OF THE BODY _____

NOUN _____

ADJECTIVE _____

NOUN _____

NOUN _____

VERB _____

ADJECTIVE _____

PLURAL NOUN _____

ADJECTIVE _____

NOUN _____

ADVERB _____

ADVERB _____

ADJECTIVE _____

MAD LIBS

ODE TO SONYA

Oh, Sonya, my _____, my furry-_____-ed love!
　　　　　　　　　　NOUN　　　　　　　　　PART OF THE BODY

Your breath is stinkier than a/an _____ from above.
　　　　　　　　　　　　　　　　　　　　　　　　NOUN

Your _____ head is larger than a baby grand, and your
　　　　ADJECTIVE

sharp claws could destroy any _____ in the land.
　　　　　　　　　　　　　　　　　　　NOUN

Just the sight of your _____ gives me such delight.
　　　　　　　　　　　　　　　　NOUN

When you smile, your pointy teeth _____ in the sun's
　　　　　　　　　　　　　　　　　　　　　　VERB

_____ light.
　　ADJECTIVE

You win the hearts and _____ of every one and all when
　　　　　　　　　　　　　PLURAL NOUN

you ride your _____ bicycle that is much too small.
　　　　　　　　ADJECTIVE

It takes a lot to impress a/an _____ such as me, but
　　　　　　　　　　　　　　　　　NOUN

you're *almost* as good-looking, which makes me _____ happy.
　　　　　　　　　　　　　　　　　　　　　　　　ADVERB

To some, a lemur and a bear in love is _____ strange.
　　　　　　　　　　　　　　　　　　　ADVERB

But, my _____ Sonya, I love you just the same.
　　　　　　　ADJECTIVE

From MADAGASCAR 3 MAD LIBS®. Madagascar 3 © 2012 DreamWorks Animation L.L.C. Published by
Price Stern Sloan, an imprint of Penguin Group (USA) Inc., 345 Hudson Street, New York, NY 10014.

MAD LIBS® is fun to play with friends, but you can also play it by yourself! To begin with, DO NOT look at the story on the page below. Fill in the blanks on this page with the words called for. Then, using the words you have selected, fill in the blank spaces in the story.

Now you've created your own hilarious MAD LIBS® game!

TRAIN TOUR

PERSON IN ROOM _____

ADJECTIVE _____

NOUN _____

ADJECTIVE _____

VERB ENDING IN "S" _____

ADJECTIVE _____

ADJECTIVE _____

ADJECTIVE _____

NOUN _____

VERB ENDING IN "ING" _____

PERSON IN ROOM _____

NOUN _____

ADJECTIVE _____

VERB _____

VERB ENDING IN "S" _____

MAD LIBS®

TRAIN TOUR

Buon giorno, _____! Why don't you come aboard
<u>PERSON IN ROOM</u>

the Circus Zaragoza train for a/an _____ tour? This
<u>ADJECTIVE</u>

train is where all the _____ happens. We travel from
<u>NOUN</u>

city to _____ city aboard the Zaragoza Express, and
<u>ADJECTIVE</u>

all the circus eats, sleeps, and _____ here. First
<u>VERB ENDING IN "S"</u>

let me show you where Vitaly, the _____ tiger, lives.
<u>ADJECTIVE</u>

Hello, Vitaly! Look, he is eating his _____ borscht.
<u>ADJECTIVE</u>

Oh, he doesn't look too happy to see our _____ faces.
<u>ADJECTIVE</u>

My apologies, Vitaly! We'll leave you to your _____.
<u>NOUN</u>

Next is the terrier train car. The silly little doggies are fighting and

_____. Talk about a/an _____ complex!
<u>VERB ENDING IN "ING"</u> <u>PERSON IN ROOM</u>

Next up is Gia's car. Oops, we caught her talking to her own

_____ in the mirror. She does that sometimes. Finally
<u>NOUN</u>

we are at the _____ Circus Americano train car! Alex,
<u>ADJECTIVE</u>

Melman, Gloria, and Marty _____ here. They are
<u>VERB</u>

circus and we are circus, and circus _____ together!
<u>VERB ENDING IN "S"</u>

MAD LIBS® is fun to play with friends, but you can also play it by yourself! To begin with, DO NOT look at the story on the page below. Fill in the blanks on this page with the words called for. Then, using the words you have selected, fill in the blank spaces in the story.

Now you've created your own hilarious MAD LIBS® game!

FOR BETTER
OR FOR BORSCHT

NOUN _____

A PLACE _____

ADJECTIVE _____

ADJECTIVE _____

ADJECTIVE _____

PLURAL NOUN _____

ADVERB _____

ADVERB _____

TYPE OF LIQUID _____

VERB _____

NOUN _____

TYPE OF LIQUID _____

NOUN _____

ADJECTIVE _____

NOUN _____

NOUN _____

ADJECTIVE _____

MAD LIBS®
FOR BETTER
OR FOR BORSCHT

Borscht is a favorite _____ of me, Vitaly. Recipe is best in
                            NOUN

Russia and in all (the) _____. No one makes borscht
                            A PLACE

like _____ Vitaly. But you can try.
        ADJECTIVE

Chop a/an _____ onion and a few _____
               ADJECTIVE   ADJECTIVE

carrots. Then peel the _____ of two beets and cut them
                            PLURAL NOUN

up _____. Place the vegetables _____
        ADVERB   ADVERB

into boiling _____, and let them _____
               TYPE OF LIQUID   VERB

for twenty minutes. Then add one tablespoon freshly churned

_____, two cups canned _____, some very
   NOUN   TYPE OF LIQUID

finely shredded _____, and a dash of vinegar. Allow the
                      NOUN

_____ mixture to simmer. When ready, pour borscht
   ADJECTIVE

carefully into bowls and add a dollop of sour _____ and
                                                    NOUN

grated _____. Serve immediately. Like revenge, borscht
            NOUN

is best served _____.
                   ADJECTIVE

MAD LIBS® is fun to play with friends, but you can also play it by yourself! To begin with, DO NOT look at the story on the page below. Fill in the blanks on this page with the words called for. Then, using the words you have selected, fill in the blank spaces in the story.

Now you've created your own hilarious MAD LIBS® game!

GIA'S DREAMS

PLURAL NOUN _____

PLURAL NOUN _____

NOUN _____

ADJECTIVE _____

NOUN _____

EXCLAMATION _____

VERB _____

VERB _____

NOUN _____

NOUN _____

VERB _____

NOUN _____

PART OF THE BODY _____

ADJECTIVE _____

ADJECTIVE _____

PART OF THE BODY (PLURAL) _____

ADJECTIVE _____

NOUN _____

MAD LIBS®

GIA'S DREAMS

Ladies and gentle-_____, boys and _____,
PLURAL NOUN   PLURAL NOUN

may I have your undivided _____, please? It is
NOUN

my pleasure to present myself, Gia, the _____ jaguar
ADJECTIVE

and incredible trapeze _____ extraordinaire! A jaguar
NOUN

trapeze artist, you say? _____! Impossible! You'll have to
EXCLAMATION

_____ it to believe it! Just watch me as I _____
VERB   VERB

through the _____ with the greatest of ease! I defy the laws
NOUN

of _____ as I flip and I _____ from one trapeze
NOUN   VERB

_____ to the next using nothing but my paws, my tail,
NOUN

and my _____. It's incredible! It's _____! It's
PART OF THE BODY   ADJECTIVE

the most _____ thing you've ever seen with your
ADJECTIVE

own two _____! Encore, you say? As you wish, my
PART OF THE BODY (PLURAL)

_____ audience. After all, the _____ must go on!
ADJECTIVE   NOUN

MAD LIBS® is fun to play with friends, but you can also play it by yourself! To begin with, DO NOT look at the story on the page below. Fill in the blanks on this page with the words called for. Then, using the words you have selected, fill in the blank spaces in the story.

Now you've created your own hilarious MAD LIBS® game!

TRAPEZE AMERICANO, BY ALEX

ADJECTIVE _____

ADVERB _____

ADJECTIVE _____

NOUN _____

PLURAL NOUN _____

NOUN _____

NOUN _____

NOUN _____

NOUN _____

PART OF THE BODY _____

NOUN _____

VERB _____

NOUN _____

PART OF THE BODY _____

NOUN _____

NOUN _____

ADJECTIVE _____

PART OF THE BODY _____

MAD LIBS®
TRAPEZE AMERICANO, BY ALEX

So, Gia, you want to learn the _____ ways of Trapeze
                                    ADJECTIVE

Americano? All right, listen up and listen _____.
                                              ADVERB

First, you must understand the _____ science behind
                                  ADJECTIVE

Trapeze Americano—like the velocity of the _____
                                               NOUN

and the laws of _____ and how to calculate the
                   PLURAL NOUN

square _____ of the _____ divided by the
         NOUN   NOUN

_____. Got it? Okay. So in Trapeze Americano you
   NOUN

don't work with another _____. That's right—you
                            NOUN

must catch your own _____ in midair! Sometimes this
                       PART OF THE BODY

involves grabbing onto the _____ with your teeth. And
                              NOUN

don't _____ if you miss the trapeze bar. You can simply
         VERB

bounce off the _____ if you are so inclined or slam your
                  NOUN

_____ into a/an _____ for added effect.
PART OF THE BODY   NOUN

You will probably end up with a bruised _____ or a/an
                                           NOUN

_____ eye. Trapeze Americano is not for the faint
   ADJECTIVE

of _____!
      PART OF THE BODY

MAD LIBS® is fun to play with friends, but you can also play it by yourself! To begin with, DO NOT look at the story on the page below. Fill in the blanks on this page with the words called for. Then, using the words you have selected, fill in the blank spaces in the story.

Now you've created your own hilarious MAD LIBS® game!

THE GREATEST SHOW ON EARTH!

PERSON IN ROOM _____

ADJECTIVE _____

PLURAL NOUN _____

NOUN _____

VERB ENDING IN "ING" _____

NOUN _____

VERB ENDING IN "ING" _____

NOUN _____

PLURAL NOUN _____

ADJECTIVE _____

ADJECTIVE _____

VERB _____

NOUN _____

ADJECTIVE _____

A PLACE _____

PLURAL NOUN _____

A PLACE _____

ADJECTIVE _____

MAD☻LIBS®
THE GREATEST SHOW ON EARTH!

_____ presents . . .

PERSON IN ROOM

The All-_____ , All-Animal Circus Extravaganza!

ADJECTIVE

Come one, come _____ for never-before-scene acts

PLURAL NOUN

of bravery and _____! You'll see:

NOUN

• a tightrope-_____ giraffe and hippopotamus!

VERB ENDING IN "ING"

• a sea lion and a zebra shooting themselves out of a/an _____!

NOUN

• a jaguar on the _____ trapeze!

VERB ENDING IN "ING"

• chimps playing songs with a/an _____!

NOUN

• tiny toy _____ on roller skates!

PLURAL NOUN

These and many more _____ wonders await you at the

ADJECTIVE

All-Animal Circus Extravaganza! Critics call this _____

ADJECTIVE

performance a "must-_____ event" and "the _____

VERB   NOUN

of the year!" The show goes on Saturday under the _____

ADJECTIVE

big top in (the) _____. _____ are on sale now

A PLACE   PLURAL NOUN

at your local (the) _____. Buy them now before it's

A PLACE

too _____!

ADJECTIVE

From MADAGASCAR 3 MAD LIBS®. Madagascar 3 © 2012 DreamWorks Animation L.L.C. Published by
Price Stern Sloan, an imprint of Penguin Group (USA) Inc., 345 Hudson Street, New York, NY 10014.

MAD LIBS® is fun to play with friends, but you can also play it by yourself! To begin with, DO NOT look at the story on the page below. Fill in the blanks on this page with the words called for. Then, using the words you have selected, fill in the blank spaces in the story.

Now you've created your own hilarious MAD LIBS® game!

I'M STILL ALEX FROM THE ROCK

ADJECTIVE _____

NOUN _____

PLURAL NOUN _____

ADJECTIVE _____

NOUN _____

NOUN _____

PLURAL NOUN _____

ADJECTIVE _____

VERB _____

ADJECTIVE _____

VERB (PAST TENSE) _____

PLURAL NOUN _____

NOUN _____

VERB _____

NOUN _____

ADJECTIVE _____

NOUN _____

SAME NOUN _____

MAD LIBS®
I'M STILL ALEX FROM THE ROCK

The New York Zoo is my home, _____ home. My rock,
_____ADJECTIVE

in my enclosure, is where I was on top of the _____.
_____NOUN

_____ came from far and wide just to hear me roar
PLURAL NOUN

my _____ roar. I had not a/an _____ in
_____ADJECTIVE_____NOUN

the world. Life was fun and _____-free. The people fed
_____NOUN

me more raw _____ than I could ever eat. Everything
_____PLURAL NOUN

was laid out on a/an _____ platter. I could just sit
_____ADJECTIVE

back and _____ and have a/an _____ time.
_____VERB_____ADJECTIVE

And now my friends expect me to give up everything that I've

_____ for to run off with the circus? I mean, sure, I
VERB (PAST TENSE)

met some pretty awesome new _____ along the way—
_____PLURAL NOUN

Vitaly, Stefano, and Gia. And yes, my zoo friends were having the

_____ of their lives. So was I, now that I _____
NOUN_____VERB

about it. I guess the truth is, a life of _____ and ease
_____NOUN

means nothing without my _____ friends by my side.
_____ADJECTIVE

Maybe the circus _____ is the _____
_____NOUN_____SAME NOUN

for me after all.

MAD LIBS® is fun to play with friends, but you can also play it by yourself! To begin with, DO NOT look at the story on the page below. Fill in the blanks on this page with the words called for. Then, using the words you have selected, fill in the blank spaces in the story.

Now you've created your own hilarious MAD LIBS® game!

VITALY'S VALIANT RETURN

ADJECTIVE _____

A PLACE _____

ADJECTIVE _____

ADJECTIVE _____

PLURAL NOUN _____

VERB ENDING IN "ING" _____

A PLACE _____

ADJECTIVE _____

NOUN _____

PART OF THE BODY _____

PLURAL NOUN _____

TYPE OF LIQUID _____

NOUN _____

NOUN _____

VERB (PAST TENSE) _____

NOUN _____

ADJECTIVE _____

NOUN _____

MAD LIBS®

VITALY'S VALIANT RETURN

This circus critic had the _____ pleasure of attending
                                    ADJECTIVE

the all-animal circus in (the) _____ last night. The
                                    A PLACE

event was _____ from start to finish, but the highlight
                ADJECTIVE

of the evening was the _____ return of Vitaly the
                                ADJECTIVE

Russian tiger. Many _____ ago, Vitaly was known
                            PLURAL NOUN

for his skill at _____ through a teeny, tiny hoop.
                    VERB ENDING IN "ING"

People came from all over (the) _____ to witness this
                                        A PLACE

_____ feat. But one fateful _____, Vitaly
        ADJECTIVE   NOUN

missed the hoop and lit his _____ on fire. After that,
                                PART OF THE BODY

Vitaly stopped jumping through _____. But last night,
                                        PLURAL NOUN

Vitaly returned to glory when he proudly walked into the big

top, covered himself in _____, and ran toward the
                                TYPE OF LIQUID

miniature _____. He leaped, and in the blink of a/an
                NOUN

_____, he had _____ through the little
        NOUN   VERB (PAST TENSE)

hoop! The _____ went wild. Vitaly was back and more
                NOUN

_____ than ever. It was truly a/an _____ for the ages.
    ADJECTIVE   NOUN

MAD LIBS® is fun to play with friends, but you can also play it by yourself! To begin with, DO NOT look at the story on the page below. Fill in the blanks on this page with the words called for. Then, using the words you have selected, fill in the blank spaces in the story.

Now you've created your own hilarious MAD LIBS® game!

MORT THE CIRCUS PERFORMER, BY MORT

NOUN _____

NOUN _____

NOUN _____

ADJECTIVE _____

NUMBER _____

ADJECTIVE _____

ADJECTIVE _____

ADJECTIVE _____

PERSON IN ROOM _____

ADVERB _____

ADJECTIVE _____

EXCLAMATION _____

A PLACE _____

If *I* were in charge of the circus, it would be the most adorable

_____ you've ever seen! It would be a one-_____
　　　NOUN　　　　　　　　　　　　　　　　　　　　　　　　　　　NOUN

show starring *ME* and only *ME*! To start, I would face a flaming

_____, just like Vitaly. Except instead of jumping
　　　　NOUN

through it, I would give it my most _____, sad eyes to sad
　　　　　　　　　　　　　　　　　　　　ADJECTIVE

those mean, old flames away! Then I would juggle _____
　　　　　　　　　　　　　　　　　　　　　　　　　　　　NUMBER

furry stuffed Mort dolls! I would go for a/an _____
　　　　　　　　　　　　　　　　　　　　　　　　　ADJECTIVE

ride on the back of Jonesy the terrier while he prances in his

_____ pink tutu! And for the _____ finale,
　ADJECTIVE　　　　　　　　　　　　　　　ADJECTIVE

_____ would shoot me out of a cannon, and I would
PERSON IN ROOM

fly _____ into a pool of _____, fluffy
　　　ADVERB　　　　　　　　　　　　　ADJECTIVE

bunnies! _____! It would be the cutest show on (the)
　　　　EXCLAMATION

_____!
　A PLACE

MAD LIBS® is fun to play with friends, but you can also play it by yourself! To begin with, DO NOT look at the story on the page below. Fill in the blanks on this page with the words called for. Then, using the words you have selected, fill in the blank spaces in the story.

Now you've created your own hilarious MAD LIBS® game!

ZEBRA CANNONBALL

PART OF THE BODY _____

PLURAL NOUN _____

NOUN _____

NOUN _____

ADJECTIVE _____

NOUN _____

NOUN _____

VERB _____

VERB ENDING IN "ING" _____

ADJECTIVE _____

ADJECTIVE _____

PLURAL NOUN _____

ADJECTIVE _____

NOUN _____

NOUN _____

ADJECTIVE _____

NOUN _____

MAD LIBS®
ZEBRA CANNONBALL

When Stefano told me he wanted to shoot his own _____

PART OF THE BODY

out of a cannon, I thought he'd lost his _____. What

PLURAL NOUN

kind of crazy _____ does a thing like that? You could

NOUN

wind up in the emergency _____! Then, when Stefano

NOUN

blasted out of that _____ cannon, he missed his

ADJECTIVE

mark! Stefano ran smack into a/an _____ and was

NOUN

hanging on by a/an _____. I had to _____

NOUN   VERB

into action. I climbed right into that cannon, and Skipper

sent me _____ through the air. It was the most

VERB ENDING IN "ING"

_____ feeling in the world. I was flying like a/an

ADJECTIVE

_____ bird! I felt like I had sprouted _____.

ADJECTIVE   PLURAL NOUN

The world below me looked small and _____, and there

ADJECTIVE

I was, _____ of the sky. Once I rescued Stefano, I knew

NOUN

I'd found my true _____: a/an _____ zebra

NOUN   ADJECTIVE

cannonballer in the all-_____ circus.

NOUN

From MADAGASCAR 3 MAD LIBS®. Madagascar 3 © 2012 DreamWorks Animation L.L.C. Published by
Price Stern Sloan, an imprint of Penguin Group (USA) Inc., 345 Hudson Street, New York, NY 10014.